For Harry

M. W.

For Amy and Mike

P. D.

First published 2000 by Walker Books Ltd, 87 Vauxhall Walk, London SE11 5HJ

2 4 6 8 10 9 7 5 3 1

This book has been typeset in OPTILucius AD

Printed in Hong Kong

British Library Cataloguing in Publication Data
A catalogue record for this book is available from the British Library.

ISBN 0-7445-6780-7

Night Night, CUDDLY BEAR

Martin Waddell

illustrated by Penny Dale

WALKER BOOKS
AND SUBSIDIARIES
LONDON • BOSTON • SYDNEY

It was bedtime
and Joe started playing his
Cuddly Bear game.
"Cuddly Bear's gone somewhere,"
Joe told Mummy. "We have to ask
everyone if they've seen him."
"Everyone?" Mummy said.
"Let's start with Daddy," said Joe.

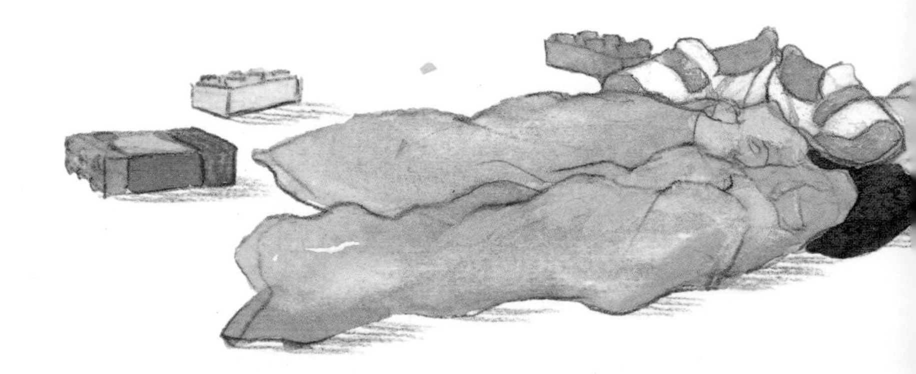

“Have you seen Cuddly Bear?”
Mummy asked Daddy.
“He’s vanished again,
just before bedtime for Joe.”

“Maybe he’s gone on a boat
to Brazil,” Daddy said.
“He knows lots of bears
there, and he’s been
learning to row.”

“I don’t think so,”
said Joe.

"Have you seen
Cuddly Bear?"
Joe asked Paul.
"He might be at
the funfair,"
Paul said.
"Cuddly Bear
likes the swings
at the fair."

"I don't think so,"
said Joe.

"Have you seen Cuddly Bear?"
Mummy asked Sarah.
"We need him now, because
Joe is going to bed."
"He might have gone to
Gran's house to climb trees,"
Sarah said. "Cuddly
Bear is a brilliant
tree-climber."

"I don't think
so," said Joe.

"No one has seen Cuddly Bear," Mummy said.
"We haven't asked everyone yet," said Joe.

Mummy asked Max the
Giraffe and Pojo and
Esmeralda but
they hadn't seen
Cuddly Bear.

"Night-night, Esmeralda.
Night-night, Pojo.
Night-night, Max,"
said Joe.

"We've asked everyone now," Mummy said.
"You haven't asked me," said Joe.
"Have you seen Cuddly Bear,
little Joe?" Mummy asked.

“He’s upstairs taking his clothes off,” Joe said.

“He’s putting on his pyjamas,” Joe said.

“He’s brushing his teeth in the bathroom,” Joe said.

“He’s in my room now, ready for bed,” Joe said.

"I can't see Cuddly Bear!" Mummy said.
"He's hiding," said Joe. "He always does this when I'm going to bed!"
"Hiding where?" Mummy said.
"You have to find him," said Joe.

"Is he in this room?" Mummy said.
"I think he must be,"
said Joe.

"Near your bed?" Mummy said.
"I think he might be,"

said Joe.

“Under your pillow?” said Mummy.
“I think he could be,” said Joe.

"Got you, Cuddly Bear!" Mummy said.
"I knew Mummy would find you,"
Joe told Cuddly Bear. "She's the
best-ever-bear-finder there is."

Joe climbed into bed beside Cuddly Bear, and Mummy told them a story, all about a small boy and his bear, who rowed all the way to Brazil. They were captured by pirates but they escaped and got home before bedtime.

"Night-night, Mummy,"
said Joe.
"Night-night, little Joe,"
Mummy said.
"Night-night, Cuddly Bear,"
whispered Joe.

And Joe and his bear
went to sleep.